Life Given

Also by Graeme Hetherington

Remote Corners (Twelvetrees Press)
In the Shadow of Van Diemen's Land (Cornford Press)

Life Given

Graeme Hetherington

Indigo

Acknowledgements

The Age, The Australian, The Canberra Times, Centoria,
Five Bells, Imago, Island, Outrider, Poetry Australia, Quadrant, Siglo,
The Sydney Morning Herald, Southerly, The Tablet, Voices, Westerly.

Life Given
ISBN 978 1 74027 143 1
Copyright © text Graeme Hetherington 2008
Copyright © cover image Michael Winters 2002
Copyright © cover design Anne Langridge 2002

An Indigo book first published 2002
Reprinted 2017

GINNINDERRA PRESS
PO Box 3461 Port Adelaide 5015
www.ginninderrapress.com.au

To the memory of James McCauley

Contents

I

West Coast, Tasmania (1)

1

Encased by buckled plywood walls
Whose window looked out on a house
As dark and ugly as our own,
We sat in silence round the fire
And got on one another's nerves,

While hung above the mantelpiece
A deer beside a mountain stream
Invited me to leave the room.
I learned to hide the joy it gave
For fear of being called a fool.

2

On visits to the family graves
My mother whistled, sang and danced
And gathered wild flowers on the way,
Arranged them till they glowed like fires

But had no warmth for us at home.
She lived behind drawn holland blinds
And never thought to fill a vase
To cheer our marble mantelpiece.

3

A wife who truly knew her place,
She wouldn't travel on the truck
That took her husband blown up from
The mine along a gravel track.
Instead she handed up his gear,

Went home and saw to other things
Like cooking and the washing up,
Left me to do the comforting,
To listen to him moan with cold
And answer when he called her name.

4

A paid up member of The Craft,
My mason-father's yarns unnerved,
Expertly timing his remarks,
That mates lopped feet off felling trees
And bludgeoned seals or tiger snakes

Thrown broken-backed on bull ant nests
Barked like a child with croup, to fall
As my young daughter wildly rode
My left until the shoe came off
Despite her whooping cough, my hiss,

Snap, shout that cudgelled love to death
While cut and stung I faced the thought
Of getting wood in with his axe
His steel-sharp cunning eyes implied
The headless horseman had once used.

5

I loved a stretch of Hell's Gate's road,
Deserted, lonely as a life,
That snaked uphill towards a brow
As proudly as a swelling cock,

That swiftly falling thrilled my crotch
Before its next sharp steep assault
Upon the sky, a fleece-soft hole
It strained to enter on its way

As in the back while father drove
And mother sat away from him
I tried, forbidden in between,
To plug the gap with fantasies.

6

I'm like my mother when I'm thin,
My father when I put on weight.
I don't like either, or myself
When I live somewhere in between,

Tormented by their presence still
As furtively I run my hands
To claim their features as my own
And wish I could be someone else.

Self-portrait

(After T.G. Wainewright)

In this room stillness is a claw curled up in silk.
Its texture is like iron filings. Any movement teases with
Images of blood and fire. Pink insides of fingers scrape
Against the grain of bristle on a face.

Flushed by wine it bursts, unquenchable with flame.
Slow rustling of rice paper scarifies the air.
Matches in a box rattle like dry undergrowth,
Sticks of furniture crackle into red.

Filmed with dust the window tensely bends
Like cellophane. A moth beats silver off its wings.
The pane is deftly slit. Fibres fly around the room.
The claw has sketched what is attached to it.

I know by heart the savagery of that feline face,
The body posturing as gentle, long-practised
And languid in deceit before it strikes.
As suave as silk it teases with what might happen next.

West Coast, Tasmania (2)

1

I turned memory up with my shoe,
A card with the name of a girl
Disfigured by hobnails and mud,
The smell of her fear as she lay

Half-hidden from view in a trench,
Pinned down and felt up by the boys,
While I was afraid of the pack
And stood as though nailed to the ground.

2

I used to keep myself awake,
Watch moonlight on my sister's hair
Turn bloody and run down her face
Of pale angelic purity
My mother wouldn't let me touch,

Or if my night-long vigil failed
I'd wake from dreams in which she died
And cross the bedroom floor to see
If I had killed her in my sleep,
Relieved if I could hear her breathe.

3

A jealous monster at her birth,
I led her with a cold damp hand
Through wet dark cuttings one mile long,

Afraid I'd push her underneath
The trains that left a yard to spare.
Today they thundered in my ears

When fast cars on a cliff-bound road
Whipped trousers back against my legs
As we walked arm in arm to town.

4

I sang the solo treble parts
In carols round the mining camps
Until my tone-deaf father came
To see me in my choirboy-dress

And sat embarrassed with his friends.
I lost my voice in *Silent Night*
And fled into the undergrowth
From his flushed face and blazing eyes,

From open fires that showed my tears
To sheepish men with three days' beard
Who either helped to improvise
Or delicately cleared their throats.

5

Touched on the raw by 'you're the odd
Man out among the lady-bards',
I lit out from the East, fled West,
A victim drawn back to the scene

Of his original defeat.
The black road licking through ravines
Opening to the solitude
Of my birthplace, grief-fertilised

I bore the boy nicknamed 'Ciss' by
Tough mining kids my mother's rough
Towelling between my legs and choice
Of lace-edged singlet, case and cape

Instead of flannel, satchel, coat,
Confirmed, as in reverse I spun
On childhood's rarely given ice-
Cream threepenny bit to our steps where,

Hell's-Gates descended cur, I clung
As she assailed with 'you're no son'
My need to thus identify
And lose, slink off, tail curled in fright

As much from bath nights as from 'Boof-
Head' waiting like the goddess-born
Achilles to resume the chase
Around our backyard rubbish tin.

The Dioskouroi

(For Gianna)

My lover for over six months,
She told me, lying back to back,
How her twin brother died: he gave,
Surgically divided, his blood

To her, then shone as a glass urn
That toppled from the mantelpiece
And smashed. Lipsticked in deepest red,
The bedroom mirror farewelled with

'We are the Dioskouroi too,
But now, please release me to him,
I've saved you for more than your share'.
I found her at last with an old

Flame butting cigarettes on her.
Scornful and superior, she
Said 'go away, you can't turn me
Into a tray full of ash', nor

Until then read, carved at birth on
Her tailbone, a joint epitaph:
'Together in death, both survive,
Deified as Zeus-flung stardust'.

West Coast, Tasmania (3)

1

A caterpillar on a branch,
The old green school bus crept along
The sixteen miles of narrow road,
And on the spare tyres in the boot

The big boys smoked and shagged in turn
A simple girl called Myrtle Dunne.
The young ones kept the drunks in hand,
Nursed plonk-filled hessian sugar sacks

That smelt of flyblown meat and dogs.
I sat between Jack Grubb and hell
The day he smashed a windowpane
To fill a glass the sky poured out

And spilt his wine-dark wasted throat.
In dreams I drove an empty bus
That turned into a chrysalis,
A butterfly that flew away.

2

'Who opened their crib?' Jack Grubb croaked,
So vile the smell, the language worse,
As decomposing from the grog
Old lags sat waiting in a van

As stuffed full as a dunny can
And closed against the morning frost
For brown-eyed catholic Kelly, called
'Cow Pat', to get his own back, blow,

Steam up, the whistle on their nerves,
Shake insides into Mickey Finns
As like a cut black snake the train
Took off with them and trucks for tin.

Hell-sickened souls, they rolled their own
And broke taboos, enthroning their
Scatology for want of hope
In jokes about their nicotine-

Stained trembling fingers bursting through
A tissue paper not as soft.
Delirious from drying out,
They fluttered underground to work

The water-running quartz that teased
Their throats as 'dry as Gabbett's arse'
Before he passed his murdered mates.
The boss's son, I felt their words

Reduce the high and low, the world
To square with their experience
As rubbish fetched up in the West
From convict days to mine earth's bowels.

3

Lying on a bed I felt my mother's shape
Grow over me. But hands said otherwise,
Confirming as they moved to keep
Reality in mind. And so the moment passed.
Psychiatry does nothing but impair

The perilously beautiful. I only know
That I became what she'd withheld.
Days of spine-snapping tension bridged
Revelations of the self. My limbs
Seized up to break, releasing me into

A room cracked open to the sky:
Deep autumn blue was backdrop for
A castle made of ice, whiter than any white
I'd seen before. Then water sang and hushed
Shadows sloping down like sides of cliffs.

All poets have a dream of being king before
Their shadow snarls around their ankle bones. I prayed
God's price would not be ruinously high.
A cloudburst, and gutters overflowed.
Through the window of a bar I saw

My body turned to faeces, swept away.
Unbelieving fingers dug at flesh to keep
Reality in mind. I wheeled around to fly.
By more than chance a woman as
Grace waited there to catch and hold me in her smile.

Touching the untouchable, she took me home.
Wave after wave of mercy rolled
Night back from day. Milk and honey flowed.
O kindly one, my pledge to you is trust.
That castle in the sky is with me yet.

4

(After William Blake's *Nebuchadnezzar*)

All the horror of the flesh
In the moist half-opened mouth
Like a wound that never heals,

In the furred and matted thighs
Of the body's swamping needs,
In the toenails turned to claws

And the thrusting on all fours,
In the inward staring eyes
Human in their fear and shame.

Van Diemen's Land

I've seldom liked the island's males,
Tamed bullies from our prison-past
Turned surly sport-champs with a grudge,
Who as remittance-men and pimps,

Touts, forger-artists, larrikins
Too sickly for a life as Ned
Became the crippled hanging-judge,
The sneaky, safely sensitive

Rich Menzies-voting poet-type,
Their women formed by alcohol,
Hulks, convictism, poverty
And church into cringe-ridden mates

As nasal as a bad violin,
Gauche, strapping lasses hard as nails,
As wooden as The Cross and sour
As vinegar to take to bed.

Plato In a Bar

Waiting for you I would look in the mirror,
Watching for you to come down the stairs
Into the bar, turning glass after glass
Of cognac around in my hands.

We would have one drink together
And leave, warming my hands in yours.
You have never come down those stairs,
And I am still looking into the mirror.

There are days when I want to live,
To smash the mirror and leave without you,
Learn how to love what is here.
You would come as I looked away,

The mirror in bits and pieces
Like treachery done to a dream.
But the mirror has claimed me forever.
One day you will come down the stairs,

Brushing the veils of cobwebs aside
With hands as white as snow.
I will turn from the mirror and see
Someone – someone the dead split image of me.

Tower

Assembled on a playing field
We looked into the morning sun
While 'Slide', The Head, a rowing man
Said crabs were caught from toilet seats,
That masturbation sent you blind

And shamed your mother's holy name.
Through half-shut eyes the whole school watched
His injured, stiff forefinger wag,
Froth fleck his old man's purple lips
As on he raved about God's wrath.

I raise my hand to shield and see
A white tower rising from the trees,
Its stone-hard length tumescent in
Pulsating light before it blows
Like Moby Dick and disappears.

West Coast, Tasmania (4)

1

Like two old gum trees shedding bark,
The miner and his wife called Neat
Because she drinks her gin that way
Grub round the peeling weatherboard

For undersized, rain-rotted spuds
To go with the tomato sauce.
Through rusty upturned water tanks
Dogs chase the chooks around the yard

Where Ernie's nailed the kero tin
For coloured ads on food and God.
The pigs he slaughters in the bath
Dry out to bacon in the lounge.

2

Unearthly in a wash of red
The city prematurely burns,
A bushfire twenty miles away
Evocative of childhood's hell,

Windborne house-blinds the shooting flames,
And charred gum leaves alighting in
Our dry Hobart backyard the same
As when I watched exploding trees

Snow on our West Coast lawn their flocks
Of darkly feathered, drunken birds,
Completing hatred's work began
By meanness forcing me, a wolf

Cub needing spuds to bake, to steal.
I left them in hot ash, forgot
While learning to tie hangman's knots
To kick the fire out on Mount Black.

3

I spent the Sunday School plate pence
To get into the match and watch
My father play for 'Labourers',
Though we were 'Staff', but living still

In fog-filled 'Town' because a war-
Time housing shortage kept us there,
From 'Hollywood' across the bridge
And up steep hills in better air.

Surveyor of pay-dirt, his foes,
Mismeasured always, true or not,
Were on his side to 'fill him in'
When packs were thick, conditions wet,

His head conceivably the ball,
While he, outsmarting, sabotaged,
Kicked out of bounds, behinds, or shins
In socks the colour of his own

And afterwards drank Menzie's health.
I also cheated on the milk
My mother, hiding from the world,
Forgot the price of for a week,

And Uncle Roy who shook the eye
Out of a needle drifted on,
The petty theft and rabbit poached
Profoundly programmed in our genes.

4

My methodist, Cain-calling gran's
And mason C of E old man's
Loud cliché-studded rows turned God
Into a knock-kneed clergyman,

A beanpole-thin, kill-joy affair
Mixed well enough in with the prim,
Scout-masterish, weak-cup-of-tea,
Politely smiling, toothy kind

For Christ to be a chip off just
One wet old block and also fail
In love to mirror my torment,
Until against their wish I went

Into a catholic home and saw
His pain-filled eyes, blood-jewelled crown
Of thorns and naked heart awash
Upon the ill-lit bedroom walls,

The life-sized crucifix behind
The door I backed into in fear.
But over-nailed, I thought, saved by
The Devil looking to his own:

'Hell's Gates' my warp and woof, the words
Made flesh like old lag Jack Grubb's plonk
That swigged snaked warmly through as I
Crept up and struck my brother down.

New Friend

I came in through the garden gate
And saw you standing thin and dark,
About to stoop and smell a rose.
Expecting me, you slowly turned

And let me truly see your face,
The blackness and the bitterness,
The savage cunning written there.
'High Priest of Evil' were the words,

The warning uttered to myself
Who had invited you to lunch
And still must welcome as a friend
And not a snake I ought to kill.

Getting There

The first drinks were like cobwebs going down,
My hand so tight around the glass I feared
Fistfuls of smithereens. Panic disappeared
With the fifth, anxiety crumpled up at eight.

Dawn broke in my head, the sun halved out
On ashen cheeks. I saw myself ten years ago
In someone trying to please an older man
Who bought straight doubles out of turn for him.

Dollar bills were slid and pressed into his hand:
A young man joined the fraternity of mates.
He caught the years up with each telescoping glass,
Two-way mirrors both were looking in.

I was the middle distance of this vignette,
Old and young enough to share both points of view:
Ageing drunks transfer their past. They kill it off.
Greedy children must know who they are.

West Coast, Tasmania (5)

Through Ocean Beach fog thick enough
For Gabbett suddenly to leap
As undernourished tree or heap
Of stones and have whatever he

Can find on me to help fill up,
The red depth marker at Hell's Gates
Like Satan's God-bequeathed cack hand
Plunged sizzling in the sea enacts

The island's history of shame,
Creating from itself a cat-
O'-nine-tails and a dripping back,
Dogs ripping out the throats of blacks,

A gallows where the broken lamp's
The lolling head, its flickering beam
The body's jig waves mirror, mock
And give no rest to as a grave.

Drenched talons fiddling prey to bits,
On days of sheerly brilliant blue
The marker savages my heart,
Shows Iocasta hanging dead,

Cut down into Ophelia drowned
With my lost children in her arms,
My English Rose destroyed by me
Avenging my source-blighted self.

A painted whore on ruined legs,
At low tide all the rot appears,
The dark beneath the scarlet coat:
Syphilitic Truganini,

Her smile light shining eerily
Upon spilt oil. All night I watch
And dream her purer than the moon,
Till dawn comes elegant and slim,

The full tide blushing with a bride,
Or turned into a red whirlwind,
Her bustle lifted ankle-high,
My crimson-footed darling twirls

With escaped cannibal-convicts
Forever in a pool of blood.
Berthed at her toe, his claw, hoof, horn,
Barbed tail, I fished, caught spiky, slimed

Flathead before forced by a squall
To climb up on the shifting shape,
Embrace my hurricane of fear:
My postmistress grandmother's stamp

I punched into hot wax and spoiled
As little devil, now Arch Fiend
With smoke-wreathed hissing Seal of State
To slam down like a Governor

And send men here; or steeple spire,
God's mark of doom pile-driven through
The water's lightning-sullied face
Where black and white-robed cormorants

And yellow-hooded gannets knifed
The crests like sacrificial priests,
Foam pouring coloured by the paint
On pillars it boiled round and peeled,

When, light gone out, gull-shrill it pitch-
Forked and despatched my soul to hell,
Re-forming to a livid, soft-
Scabbed, weeping, mutilating hand

Blue shivering flesh reflecting paired
With mine, puffed up, stained from my haul
And murders not so literal,
Exhibiting, as in a trial,

The weapons doubling for the wounds
That festered white beneath cat's-paws,
Erupted and revealed unchanged
The remnants of a Gabbett meal.

Van Diemen's Land Orchard

(For Lloyd Robson)

On the Apple Isle Satan's that tree's
Pitch-black shadow, the serpent cast down,
Unfurling and crossing an orchard in flower,
Until in retreat, all but absorbed by
The light, it re-enters, curls tighter into

The densest possible concentrate of
The past's stain; again extending, then creeping back
As God eternally nearly removes,
His tears of frustration sap on the bark
Shed more easily than He can His shame.

Stages of the Song

Horses of light, horses of dark
Gallop their opposite ways
And tear me apart.

A wind like an ice-coloured axe
Cuts through a street
And cuts me in half,

A street as straight as an arrow,
As broad as a river in flood,
One side lit, one side dark.

I stand on each side,
Light looking at dark,
Dark looking at light,

Enduring as best as I can,
Waiting for horses of light
To outstrip the horses of dark

And gallop me into a song,
Joined to the arrow-swift hurl
Of a river that sings.

West Coast, Tasmania (6)

1

Hell's Gates, where convicts knelt to fuck
Each other and for prayers before
Their nightly or eternal rest
From knotted rope or blow behind

That they might then be eaten raw,
Supplied my past, and C of E
Boys' boarding school, housemaster cruel,
Dickensian, was living proof.

A single man, descendant of
The Governor who founded Old
Nick's home on earth, the rumours flew,
Since 'Tadpole's' sugar cane beat bums

To bloody sweetness for his eyes,
And as choirmaster, organist,
Time for The Eton Boating Song,
All joy from Jesu, Joy of Man's

Desiring, till attempting to
Swat flies on boys he caught a crab
And sank us like a Tamar turd.
Nicknamed 'Blossom' by him I sang

Of ultimate sterility,
At Strahan made love the wrong way up
With English Rose to get as close
To origins as I could stand.

2

In celebrating my release
On speech night with the help of 'sweet
Nell' planted in The Albert Park,
I had the final say and drowned

The Governor's out as vomit sprayed,
Destroying prizes won to show
My hatred for the squatters' sons,
The five years given as a chance

To shut Hell's Gates. Nor did the pump
That got the poison up cut off
My head's supply of it. A small
Mine boss, my father didn't link

Housemaster 'Tadpole' with 'Bullfrog'
Sorell who spawned with Satan's sperm,
I like to think, the nick near Strahan,
Our picnic place to mark The Peace

In '45 and cause of war-
Fare breaking out in me. He scruffed
Me by the neck and croaked 'I'll strip
You bare of blossom' as he flogged

Cack-handed with his rod that spoilt
Unsparingly, not my young boy's
Point Puer-petalled back of yore,
But rose-red from outrage, my arse,

Until it bled and Matron Lord,
Old Nick's help, dressed with iodine
A well-aimed, menstruating cunt-
Bunched wound that's smarted all my life.

Mount Wellington

Bushfire-induced, abnormal trees
Sideburn and beard the Iron Duke,
Exaggerate with spectral-grey
His purple, apoplectic face
That cowers Hobart Town below

And shades transplanted English parks
Where babies lie as pillowed eyes
In royal blue prams: Vice-Regal pearls
From hoiked up oysters spat out in
A towering rage at being there.

For James McAuley

1

James McAuley was to me
What Nicholas and Narziss were to Goldmund.
I read his poems and sought him out.
Before he would agree to have me learn

He first read two or three of mine,
Ungainly things that limped and hopped about,
But desperate enough to have him pause
And let me, if I could, profit at his side.

This master craftsman, the Nicholas in him,
Saw poems worthy of the name
As pieces perfectly attained. To find again
Eternal laws was to be infinitely free;

Form was the inbuilt knowledge of a truth
As old as chaos shaped into the world.
He never said this in so many words –
His teaching was of the incidental kind,

Which brings me to the Narziss in the man.
He helped me to the bedrock of myself,
Down past the imposition of the lie
To where the one and first all-giving mother is.

A poem, he would insist, can only live
If it is born from something truly known.
God made the moon because she was of Him.
First drown in her then you will learn to swim.

2

The autumn sky is richly blue,
As deep and dark as what we know
Each dying year must bring about,
The sunlight distant, frail and chill

On leaves transparent with old age,
On children faintly touched with gold
Who blow white breath into the air
And watch it disappear like smoke.

3

The window frame against the blind
Has made a cross as black as death,
A bird that hovers by my head
On long stiff wings that never flap,

And when I make him fly I learn
That out of sight's not out of mind
As darkness deep within green pines
Spreads slowly out to overwhelm.

4

The rose has left her sheltered bed
To flower beyond the picket fence,
Her tall thin stem and gorgeous head
A question mark that overhangs

A strip of melting asphalt path
That gleams like water in a pool,
Like polish on a thick black boot
That breaks her gently asking face.

5

Dark suits crumpled, slept in the night before,
Mourners stole the show, risen from the dead.
In place of armbands tennis socks
Flashed out from trousers worn half-mast,

But at the rear of the cathedral stood
Two women veiled, dressed splendidly in black,
The convict and the lady theme
Alive and well in Hobart Town.

6

Limbs bent, foliage flat,
Drawn together as in pain,
Trees print themselves upon
A smudged blue winter sky.

Sleet-grey rolling clouds
Obliterate deep porticos
And palace hallways,
Shatter them to bits of blue,

Swallow up and bear away
Each impress of each tree.
But darkening storm winds drive
Pine quills sharp as nails

Until the sun must know and rise,
Be seen to climb and build
From the centre of its sky
A castle made of gold and blue.

7

Again I have dreamt of you dead,
Leaf-thin on the softening ground,
Your skin drying out like a snake's
That fluttered as gently I kissed

Then woke without seeing you rise.
Today as I cut the long grass,
Uncovering things rotting and damp,
I choked on the taste of black earth.

West Coast, Tasmania (7)

I came across a tiger snake
The shape and colour of the road,
As still and silent as the day.
Instinctively I sought to kill
And stick in hand disguised myself

Among the tense, expectant trees,
My arm a heavy branch that fell
And flew to splinters as I struck,
Repeatedly, relentlessly
My shadow into blood and dust.

Hobart Town Chiaroscuro

1

The light is clear, the shadows dark,
And wind upon the water's face,
Among the silvered poplar trees
And long grass dried out in the fields

Excites the language of the soul:
An unscarred, deep, pre-settlement
Blue sky and sun declining fast
Intensely painful to behold.

2

The garden sleeps in green and grey,
Hydrangea heads in russet heaps
Like dead tea leaves upon the path,
But rose, camellia, jonquil flower,

Surprise me with their random song,
And round the corner as I climb
The rhododendron's outstretched arms
Are red with bursts of brilliant flame.

3

A landscape from Cézanne's last years
Once opened to my eyes and gave
An old man seated by himself,
Dear death the friend he waited for,

An image that I've wondered at
Until today it came alive:
A blackbird singing here and there
Searched for me in an empty park.

4

The sun had shone all summer long
Till life was just as sure as death,
Then autumn without warning signs
Was there one morning when I woke,

A greyness clamped on to the sky
As stunned with disbelief I rose
And felt the tiredness in my limbs,
My heart beneath my casual hand.

5

Another stunning, soul-wide day,
The ineffable Blackman's Bay
Will not stay so for long. Grey clouds
Inevitably shadow-stain

A scene too beautiful for me.
A man snarls at a crippled dog
That cringes, whines, curls up and begs
Deep down inside, like me, for death.

6

Waves toss a silver coin about,
Expand, crush, elongate and break
Light into crazy mirror shapes,
Run every treasure ship aground
And bounce a ball into the sky.

7

In parks that kings in stone by now
Must share with ordinary folk
By day at least, old men might touch
In shuffling past their hats without

First straightening backs and looking up,
Since after all they only have
In common stiffening on, not in-
To marble slabs. At dead of night,

When tar-black iron gates in glass-
Spiked walls are locked on emptiness
That can't offend, deep-frozen eyes
Rolled skyward thaw back into place.

8

The westward hills are cleared to light
And sprinkled with fine dust of gold,
The shadows slipping further down

Like rings of night cast off by day,
The sea of black around the base
At low tide waiting for the turn.

The Sins of the Fathers

(For G.B.)

You blew your brains out, spattered blood
On books I'd lent: *The Tree of Man*,
Paradise Lost, *Howard's End*, *For
the Term of His Natural Life*,

An Addam's album of cartoons.
I wondered at their role, and mine,
Our boozing, if they'd somehow caused
Endogenous depression to

Intensify, explode your wits.
More likely great grandfather hanged
In irons for murdering a black
Wants nothing added to account

For need to be released, except
Time lived in shame, as stains glimpsed on
The spines for years explains their spread
To my mind's eye that triggered this.

Restless

1

Footsteps sound and I dream that you will come,
Fashioned out of literature and those
Real people of my unrequited loves,
Nameless One, with no face to love you by.

Composites are shapeless, footsteps fade away.
Dreams briefly live, but just as briefly die.
New footsteps sound their promise to complete –
Nameless One, with no face to love you by.

2

It's there as something spoken, never said,
As something given but withheld.
It's always there, if only to elude,

As with Narcissus when he reached.
I've never understood, and yet I would
Hold water in my hand and keep it if I could.

3

The hammer fell into the dark
Between the chimney and the wall,
Refused the glitter of a hook
Revolving on a piece of string,

But not the hope I also cast
With one for luck into the hole,
As glinting on my line it rose
To nail the roof with moon and stars.

4

Glass-surfaced waves break to spray
Across the road. Our warmth weaves through
A frozen world, and safely home,
Hail ricocheting off the roof,
It is the closest we have been:
Huge mirrors rise before the reef
Then waves are like white roses blown.

5

Into your hands I will give
A butterfly shell barely hinged
From a perilous, wind-buffeted flight

Among the tall storm-broken flowers
And a stone as a sign
For a heart that will mend.

6

A stretch of water breathtaking in its calm,
A wealth of carpet laid from shore to shore,
The rainbow with its unbroken reach,
All speak of Peter having walked

Towards another whom he loved.
I see the world this way because of us
Who throw flat stones and make them skip:
Love's miracle is that it can be real.

7

Days of terror, joy and doubt,
There is a pure stream and a dark
And one that's intermixed with both

Flowing through me every waking hour.
It's bearable because you flower
Beside me in the wilderness.

8

In this garden soft winds blow,
Sunlight settles like a claim,
Spreads through each and every tree,

Telling us our love is strong,
Dandelion and cabbage moth
As splendid as the wild red rose.

9

I dreamt I forked our garden bed
And caught the Devil on a prong,
And though I tried to shake him free
He slid a little further on,

Until you struck him off in rage,
Impatient with the silly game,
His ever-changing, subtle hold,
My half-wish not to see him gone.

10

A fine-looking pitcher that leaks,
An oven that lets in the cold,
Inanna first tempts then destroys,
Leads stallions to tread in the pool

And muddy the water they drink,
Embraces the lion with a net
Stretched over the pit she has dug,
And walks past my window in spring.

11

Love's as thin as smiles are thin
When the spade cuts through the root,
When trees have bled to death and there's

No thought to save from winter's grip,
Is as deep as smiles are deep
When the rose and thorn are one.

12

Last spring a blackbird built a nest
In our cotoneaster tree.
It's empty as a ruin now,
But in the mist red berries drip

As from an old wound opened to
Remind us of our gain. Today
The night took wing and flew in with
A twig announcing winter's end.

13

Firetails like matches struck go out
On entering green-golden pines
So purely straight and upwards drawn

They soar like glowing shafts across
Blue gardens where white roses drift
Their petals round a nest in flames.

14

Red hot pokers in the garden speak
Of comets bearing down on earth.
Dry stubble prints the story on bare feet.
Leaves crackle and shrivel up.
They sound like cinders underfoot.

15

I saw an angel's glittering wings
At rest upon a patch of sea
But lost them in the endless grey

As sun set through the falling leaves.
Downcast, I tried all vantage points
Till every chance had flown away.

16

His latest kingdom weighs heavily on him.
He paces out the garden planning to divide.
Snow whispers as it settles on the roof.
Too often in the past he has inclined

To winter voices in favour of the cold.
Discord has bred a monolith of ice.
At least this one has read the blank sheet that he is.
She even offers peace: 'Unhappy though I am,

I cannot thaw my heart enough to speak'.
Nor he, as ice cracks in the guttering.
Shared winter voices are warmer than outside.
There could be dangers in trying to divide.

17

The waves are fluent with my love,
The flow of moonlight catching in dark hair.
Star-woven crests hold her for a time:
A woman of European bearing walks,

The corners of a cliff following her round.
But dreams like waves can only break,
Each sounds its slap across my face,
The corners sharper than before.

18

Restless, seeking always everywhere
For miracles of images to bring
God home from His vast emptiness,

Home never home save when they're found,
Today the stained glass windows round
Glorious sunflowers for His eyes.

West Coast, Tasmania (8)

1

They haunt me still, the derelicts,
Those sad-eyed alcoholic men
Who lost whatever jobs they found
Around the West Coast mining towns.
And I'm drunk in another way,

On poetry that also wrecks
But leaves you richer at the end,
Like one of those old single blokes
Who managed out of frying pans
And saw God on the fire-lit walls.

2

From hills above Trial Harbour where
I walk hot and bothered by huge
Iridescent blowies evolved
From the cannibal shit of Pearce
And Gabbett flogged raw and thus in

Dire need of salt caked on my face,
Waves hemming, gulls stitching with white
The sweep of Madonna-blue cloak
Look cool. Soul-imperilled by how
The past's worked itself out in me,

They increase my thirst till I gulp
Air feathery as angels' wings,
And feel, black sombrero tipped back
To mop up hate sweated, my Hell's
Gate's head try the sun on for size.

II

Europe (1)

1

It hurts to be always the guest,
The unwanted stranger who eats
And sleeps in another man's house.
He welcomes with water as much

To steady my nerves as quench thirst,
Refrains from enquiries at first
But finally asks for my name,
Birthplace, occupation and age

If he feels familiar enough.
The worst are the questions withheld,
The quick wondering looks as they shift
And offer a place in the group,

Make room at the table and share
The food barely covering plates.
Will he use his knife to cut meat
Or our tongues and eyes from our heads

For wagging and staring too long?'
This evening from the dark yard,
Unable to join in I watched
The family happily talk,

Light flooding their faces with warmth
And panic my mind as I took
A tree in my arms and was home,
Night nailing me there with the stars.

2

(After a painting by George Iakovides, Athens)

I've never seen such happiness,
Such joy as these Greek children show
Who blow their whistles and their flutes,
Beat kettle drums and play violins

With all the energy they've got,
Their heads thrown back and legs stretched out,
Eyes glistening with a wild delight
As desperately they keep in time,

Resist the chaos of their souls,
Unmindful of a glowing tree
With flowers like a fall of snow,
The clock as truthful as a skull.

3

I've woken feeling tired. It's difficult to rise,
Like Michelangelo's prisoners in stone,
Half-surfaced, half-wanting to rejoin
Their flawless dream of natural shape and line.

But one is more at rest. His bed is soft.
He's still part of a hill remembering waterfalls,
The clutch of roots and wedging sun that fashioned him.
I too would be released and sink more deeply in.

4

I love this Rembrandt most, the wisps of beard
And quietly folded hands, the hint of cloak and chair.
At least two thirds is background and it's black,

Most of the clothing too. Some of the face,
Faintly skeletal, the eyes rheum-filled and soft,
Has been lost to the dark, the curtain nearly drawn.

West Coast, Tasmania (9)

1

Emerging from the dunes the queers
Flash cocks at men who walk alone.
Why not, I wonder, on my way,
Bored stiff and womanless for months,
To swim among and perv upon

The inaccessible Greek girls
And topless tourists round the bay,
Have random, casual sex and get
The dirty water off my chest?
No need can rout my fear of men

Descended from Hell's Gate's old lags
With threepence in one hand and string
Fluttering undone from their flies,
Their whiskered wet red drunkards' mouths,
My father calling the police.

2

In Florence, in a dream, a man-
Sized blood-and-mud-bespattered thing
Crouched waiting in a room for me
As in my Goya print where hair

Obscures the bowed, chained figure's face.
It rose full-view to be Jack Grubb,
A West Coast bender-bust old lag
Obscenely begging for a job

From my old man Pig Iron Bob hooked
So thoroughly he thought his roots
Grubbed out and ran the Renison,
Bell-gone, 'no liability'

Tin mine. I stabbed and stabbed at Jack,
As on and on he came at me,
Unbuttoning and slobbering,
At his arse-weeping shamelessness

No European peasant wit
Or convict-cunning could redeem,
And all the wounds I knew were one,
And mine, as Hell's Gates opened wide.

3

Postmaster in a Hydro town
A day's bus ride from any girls,
My homosexual Uncle Max
Was hounded out by gangs of males,

His wavy hair and lisping voice,
His mincing walk and mauve silk scarves,
The way he slowly licked a stamp,
The peppermint upon his breath,

His soft pink useless-looking hands
Like rotten fruit about to fall,
Too much in nineteen fifty four
When men dammed water and themselves.

4

A member of a swarm of bees,
Not poor and certainly not rich,
My father's like the market Greeks
Who dodge around Omonia Square

On business till the day they die.
Forever in a coat and hat,
Not necessarily a tie,
They walk about in company,

Take sudden leave and rush to meet
Another group for talk and drinks.
I've never seen one by himself
Just quietly sit and read a book.

5

For Dr Ivana Gajdosová

Madonna-blue and golden in
The dress I bought, you wore it from
The shop in heavily stone-walled,
Volcanically-imperilled, dark

Catania, as map in hand
You led through decadent baroque,
Cramped, twisting, Cosa Nostra streets
Attractive to my Hell's Gate's soul,

Held high The Cross and petrified
The workings of a viper's nest
A public-toilet queer unfroze
That evening, when as Theseus

Alone I hit the bull's eye of
Despair not with my tempted sword
But with my vision of you as
The fire of love preceding me.

Europe (2)

1

Piero's barefoot peasant girls sing praise,
Their smiles brushed on by tips of angels' wings,
And Mary kneeling has earth-mother thighs,

Her face an eggshell white as she adores.
A great brown cow looks on, its soft liquescent eyes
Splintering to a crucifix of stars.

2

The old Dominican with hound-of-heaven teeth
Is gaunt and pointed like a Gothic arch,
And in the Gondi Chapel Brunelleschi's Christ

Bleeds always for the one and only God.
Strong voices chant and softly melt away.
My cringing flesh tries on the feel of fire.

3

Girls sing like spring's first waters running free.
One plays the mandolin. It softens stone
And thaws the cold. Masaccio's life

Of Peter martyred glows more deeply red,
The hems of garments stitched bright gold
To thrill our blood, free flesh from winter's hold.

4

Ravenna's fallen asleep under snow.
Only the roads and railways are dark,
Dark as the comings and goings of men

Absolved for loving the good enough to
Piece together Christ's life with mosaics,
His coming and going white as the storm.

5

Corpse-grey melting snow and ice
Return the city to a swamp,
Have me spend the day beneath

A dome that's rescued buried life,
Where the Saint spreads wide his arms
And welcomes into paradise.

6

The fields around the convent shine,
Ablaze with early morning frost.
Teresa walked the blistering cold
And ached for warmth against the walls

Washed whiter than the winter sun.
The golden child upon the stairs
Has led her to another home:
Life's like one night at some bad inn.

7

The bier conveying Jesus dead
Through ice-black, rigid streets dissolved
The crowd's restraint. Its swaying timed
To muffled drum beats and a chant

As old as breathing in and out,
It caught the rhythm of the heart,
Rich priestly robes worn casually
Since triumph was assured. A life

Out in the cold, I also cracked,
The seasons now the right way round,
Snow dark-edged as a mourning card
The thaw beginning flecked with flowers.

8

Hands faintly touching her white breasts,
The small Madonna with eyes closed
Smiles peacefully into the sun,

Luxuriating in the warmth.
This gentle creature is the spring,
The resurrection and the life.

Beyond her dreaming, blissful face,
The pleasing news for all to share,
She has the certainty of stone,

A halo light, but cast in iron,
A foot to tread the serpent out,
Ecstasy requiring strength to bear.

9

A refuge from the squalid town,
The monastery is loved by nuns
Because their husband lives at home

Instead of in the coffee bars.
For Him they weed the Easter flowers,
Bruise-coloured pansies and the rose

With petals like a healthy wound,
Red poppies with their hard black scabs,
Light-scarred, soul-white chrysanthemums.

10

All the goodness of the world
In the story of His trial,
In His loyalty to the stone

Staring at the noonday sun,
In His eyes that could withstand
Opening on the heart of light,

In the trust that would not test
Whether God might save or not,
In the pure thought winging high

Above all need for living here,
Above all fear for limb and life,
In the knowledge that we rise,

In the blazing blue of sky,
In the desert bared to gold,
While the kingdoms of this world

Fell away before His eyes,
Stone-grey eyes that opened on
The kingdom risen in His heart.

West Coast, Tasmania (10)

1

Near done from breaking in stiff shoes
In Barcelona's summer heat,
I think of how my grandad Old
Bob Taylor died while lying on

A bench outside the Bookie's Club,
Although he'd just bet two each way
And heel and toe protectors flashed.
My gamble to exhaust Hell's Gate's

Insatiably pursuing hounds
On foot, or with a poem from streets
Fouled by real dogs throw them off scent,
Thus lost, my soul collapsed to ash,

Reducing me to risk without
Apotropaic steel, a sleep
Upon a park seat, praying that
I'd wake with poison-baited lines.

2

Yes, I remember Hobart Town,
I lived there in another life
As Gabbett who ate human flesh
In order to escape Hell's Gates,

The horrors of the Wild West Coast,
In preference for the capital.
My consciousness still bears the scars
And colours everything I see,

The people with their crippled souls
And physical ungainliness,
The streets of toyland cottages
Beneath the ponderous expanse

Of Wellington, a name that rubs
The local aristocracy's
Snub nose into the convict dirt
And barely lets the city breathe.

3

In Copenhagen Harbour hangs
A wrecked ship's bell in memory,
Its cold stiff tongue as silenced by
The welder's flame as convicts' were

By rope. I tug a piece and join
Them dislocated in their head-
Without-a-body dance upon
Dutch Tasman's nearby grave, because

He set in logbook entries on
Van Diemen's Land's West Coast the fire
The English lit and flesh-fuelled to
The roaring fury of Hell's Gates,

And fingering my neck I see
A red depth marker as a wound,
The Little Mermaid green with rust
As Truganini sickening.

4

Broad-arrow patterns in the brick
Courtyard before Charlottenberg,
Four men whipped on in chains beneath
A well-horsed emperor, the world

Is still a prison as I stroll
On parole from Van Diemen's Land,
My past intensifying yet,
More deeply etched the more I try

To further distance it, escape
Time running backwards to my cell,
A cold antipodean womb
Within the shadow of Hell's Gates.

5

God's unevaporated tear,
Named for the Devil from the start,
The ineluctably sad isle,
Melancholic, alcoholic

From genocide and convict days
Contaminates my blood as song,
A bitter, soul-dark, harsh complaint.
Black hulk to starboard all my life,

I threw my harpoon and engaged
Too deeply to escape my poem
Now luring me through northern seas,
The same that sank me in the south

As an apprentice Ahab, maimed
In my encounter near Hell's Gates,
My unwept childhood frozen hard
Into a precious hoard of grief.

Europe (3)

1

You've seen all manner of men fall,
My silver-grey, shade-bearing tree,
At night like Jesus kneeling on
Stones sharp and cold as myriad-

Eyed God's cruelly appraising face,
Drought-blunted blades of grass the nails
And spear to soon try piercing Him
For any sap He might have left,

The wooden props as rotten as
His twenty centuries-old limbs,
Together barely worthy of
Fire resurrecting into smoke.

2

(Eli, Eli, lema sabachthani?)

All the sadness of the world
In dying man and dying tree,
In the stone gashed to a mouth
Accusing God of dying too,

In Mary crying as she hears
The giving in, the letting go,
In John outraged at being told
What he didn't want to know.

3

The figure lithe, the hands and feet not nailed,
Arms beckoning, or left free to fly,
This Crucifixion says Christ didn't die,

But Mary knows another truth
And stares unseeing in her grief
Beyond the child she loosely holds.

4

In all his Crucifixion scenes
El Greco feminised the legs.
The knees touch as a woman's would
When in her tightly fitting skirt
She bends with slightly parted calves,

And furthermore the thighs are slim,
Quite delicately shaped and long
As in the ads for panty hose
Where all that's missing is the man
And one nail to be driven in.

5

(Pietà)

The upper half of Jesus rests
With Mary and the Saint, a group that says
Three's company, four's a crowd,

His lower half inclined towards
The other Mary turned away from them:
Overall, the baser intimacy wins.

6

It's Sunday in the capital
And tinny-sounding bells are drowned
By monstrous forty year-old cars,
The strollers in their shabby best

Too poor for even these cheap gods
That angrily destroy their church,
Drive Jesus from His pedestal
With miracles of smoke and noise.

7

With each stone slightly out of line
Or cracked, the church prays for release.
The inside smells of damp and dust
And stale tea leaves. Old women hobble past

A kneeling priest with empty eyes.
The amplifiers work too well,
Give bread and wine in mouth and throat
The sound of tall trees crashing down.

8

The homeless poor must tolerate
Not only fat rich visitors
Who loudly talk, take photographs
And put no money in the box,

But smells from damp, cracked blackened walls
Whose images have nearly gone,
The coldness and the lack of light
That save on electricity,

The rising price of candles once
Within their reach, and jokes worn thin
Among themselves about God's house
As worse than having none at all.

9

Misshapen, lonely people come and go,
Light candles, cross themselves and say a prayer
In the surroundings of a Christmas mass.
Cold comes off stone as old as God
And rain will chill them yet again,
The altar still on fire with gold.

10

The converted palace is dying of shame
And a hundred and fifty empty rooms.
The dead aspidistras won't lie down
In the courtyard grey from last month's snow,

And no one will give a crown to the king
Who sits by himself in the brocaded lounge.
The night porter yawns and it all goes dark –
Cigars, mineral water and an old brown fart.

11

The beach is like an en masse grave,
The carnage on a battlefield,
As tourists in their thousands lie
Beneath the psychopathic sun,

Their salt-encrusted, food-stuffed skins –
Rare, medium and overdone –
Embalmed in moisturising oils.
As many lie in shuttered rooms

With doors like panelled coffin lids
And rest in peace before their time,
While in the treeless, death-swept hills
Black hotel windows watch and wait.

12

A sensuously ageing town
Half-swamped in shadows thick as mud,
Luxuriant creepers bind its wounds
Or widen cracks to bring it down,

Disguise the drains with fragrant smells,
The rubbish tips with brilliant flowers,
While in the glittering pastry shops
Fat perfumed ladies are consoled.

13

Four hundred years of Turkish rule
Have left Greeks shorter, dark and fat,
Enamoured of a life of ease
And eastern inefficiency,
The shadow of their former selves

As Plato would have surely said,
Imagining his Ideal Forms,
All trace of correspondence gone,
Receding with the speed of light
Into the undreamt, furthest realms.

14

A worn medallion on a wall
Has foxed the archaeologists
Since Evans first myopically
Assigned it value in a book.
They speculate and label it

As human or a lion's head
Belonging to Venetian days,
Or going further back insist
It's Cretan if it isn't Greek,
Refuse to let time have its way,

Admit the image disappears,
Has vanished even, that it wants,
Not special pleading, but its right,
Like everything, to nothingness,
In harmony with ancient law.

West Coast, Tasmania (11)

1

Schoolteacher, spinster, WAAF returned
From islands where the Japs pack-raped,
My aunt's been missing forty years
To make her (with her brother Herb

Who for a sexual crime, lost leg,
Failed farm, divorce, bad debts and nerves
Won missing person's status too,
With sisters Dolly, Lisa, Grace,

One tranquillised, one certified,
And one, my mother, wilfully
Stone-deaf because she can't abide
The troublemaking speech begins)

A loyal member of the clan,
While I, self-exiled, language lost,
By temperament reclusive, weird,
Outraged still by a brutal past,

Feel strongly, too, the pull of blood
And search myself for signs of her
Establishing our common fate
To live destroyed, well out of sight,

Ashamed of humankind: demobbed,
She stayed in our sleep-out alone
And coughed, a shadow on her lung
My child's heart recognised had spread.

2

White sliver of a fingernail,
The moon's God's way of pointing out
His absence from the world, His trick
Of disappearing into space
While tapping into heads the news

As stale as parings on the sill
Beside which mother sat, detached,
Reclusive, abstract and remote,
A lunatic awaiting death's
Pure black perfectibility.

3

On claustrophobic summer days
My father joins me on Greek roads
That wind through towering forest trees,
Past timber mills and mining camps

Towards the beach just down below.
I hear his voice snap like a branch
From irritation with the heat,
The shovel-clinging mud from holes

That set the limit to our lives,
With me for asking where's the sea
We never came to as we searched
For winter wood upon our walks

Through thick dark horizontal scrub
Despite the promise in the name
'West Coast' when I was nine years old
And struggling for a breath of air.

4

My father drove his horse and plough
In circles lessening with the years,
More quickly finished as he aged
Until the centre disappeared,

My father glowing like the wheat,
As cheerful as a stack of hay,
As fresh and crisp as next spring's grass
That grew to stand up in his place.

5

(To The Little Mermaid, Copenhagen)

The price for having outswum conch-
Horned father Neptune's to be bound
In rusting, light-repellent bronze,
Downcast with longing on a rock,
Scared stiff in reverie and prey

Instead to tourists' outlawed touch
Without the thrilling throb in waves',
As fetching up beyond kins' reach
Has cost me dear: resisting as
A child sleep's pull, for fear, guard down,

I'd be swept through Hell's Gates and kill
From shameful love my sister in
Our shared bedroom. Iron filled my soul
That now surmounts blood's undertow,
The Devil's incest-scented bait

Disguised as letters calling home
To farewell parents close to death,
When I, self-sentenced to a life
In solitary, have just found you
To dream alive, strip bare of green,

The rot of guilt, that I at least
Might look in wonder at your flesh,
Swept through to paradise this time,
No voice or hand raised to forbid
My adoration in this form.

6

My parents' death in grand old age
At last confirmed the judgement of
My childhood heart betrayed by them.
I hear you, who were once to me,

As Gilgamesh to Enkidu,
My lost family, say 'you err'
As I reread, to find support
In precedent, *Because*, your poem

Of decent human sentiment.
But kiss withheld's an instant wound
Time turns the other cheek to. Mine
Was constant daily injury

For years in which I sensed their shame
As West Coast kids in dishing up
Hell sniffed me out as 'ciss' and 'nance',
As much if not more girl than boy

In sensibility at least.
My sister envied for her sex,
My younger brother held up as
A model for survival, I

Had no choice but to honour hate
And, down to stone, disown them all
For self strung taut, poised on a knife
Edge listening in for poetry.

Don Quixote, Segovia

1

For knights who ride across the plain
The *Alcazar* sails on a sea of trees
With sharp dark hats upon its towers,

The shortest one set at the prow
To guide the nation's ship of fools:
'Look, Sancho, yonder flies a witch!'

2

Dark rocks encrusted on facades,
The castle's pockmarked from afar,
And ravens with their satin wings

Swarm and hover near the walls
Like an escort for the ship:
'Look, Sancho, witches all wear jewels!'

3

The ravens have a frightening call
Of arrows twanging through the air,
And slate-black hats like gleaming steel

Flash shafts of light across the plain,
Explode the stones to smithereens:
'Come, Sancho, raise me from the ground.'

East Coast, Tasmania

(For Henry Reynolds)

1

Beach, sea and sky an empty stage,
Here fear of space can overwhelm,
Demand the spirit of the place
Materialise, play its part,

As when I snap around to catch
A disappearing black shape glimpsed
Out of the corner of my eye
In hunger for my stolen past.

2

The sea capricious, as deranged
As alcoholic, punch-drunk half-
Castes swilling plonk and throwing up
In gutters on a rainy day,
I need the constancy of rocks,

Walk deep into their huddled shapes
And find among them, silent, dark,
My shadow drowned, lost like the blacks,
In pools that concentrate death's stink
No new storm's risen to flush out.

3

Car tyres have scarified the sand
And Sunday strollers leave a script
As messy as the sea's is clear,
A flowing and erasing hand

Restoring the original
Of esoteric, wavy lines,
The salt-white language blacks once read
A warning in they couldn't heed.

4

Sand blowing off the dunes like smoke,
The wind in fury built and wrecked
Sphinx, obelisk and pyramid,
The dead collapsing, hollowed out,

And as I sat selecting words,
Preserving what I thought and felt,
It whipped the pencil from my hand,
Huge storm waves curling in contempt.

5

At midday in an open bay,
A wombat eating marram grass,
So unaware or unafraid

He let me stay and closely watch,
And as I walked I feared for him,
The kelp pods going off like guns.

6

A soft fat body on hard rock,
A last-gasp look around the mouth
And hollow sockets black as eyes,

Tide turned the seal this way and that
Until I pushed him further out
To hide the man-made hole that stared.

7

A great umbrella crumpled up,
Weighed down by water mixed with sand
Embedded in deep satin folds,

The black-browed albatross lies dead
Beneath the wind-thinned, feathery clouds,
Like something thrown out by the sky.

8

They came down with the mountainside,
Vast ponderous forms like dinosaurs
And brittle pterodactyl shapes,

These trees stretched out across the beach,
Their great roots stiffening in salt air
And only nature to be blamed.

9

White horses set a cracking pace
Beneath a swiftly running sky,
Beach buggies blundering on our day,

Upon the sand-spun angels' wings:
You point to an exciting line
That like a whiplash crests the dunes.

10

The sea is angry, cold and hard,
Insistent and intensely dark,
Gift-giving of a wind that bares

Dead trees like bayonets on a ridge,
Shapes marram grass and clumps of sand
To cross-cut saws and sharks' teeth bared.

11

An out-of-nowhere, keening wind
Goose-pimpling sea and sand, a vague
Unease pervades the Peron Dunes,
While from a midden's refuse blooms
Pig-face in purple, bruised flesh-tones

Reminding me of slaughtered blacks,
Tree limbs emerging sharp as flint,
As spectral as the ghosts of whites.
On such a day the unappeased
Rise up, outnumber and outwit.

12

A crime that cannot be erased,
A plant called Black Boy towers above
Sand-bitten, badly farmed grey scrub,
And cutty rushes where they hid

From flashing red hot pokers, growths
Whites utilised against their flesh,
Obey if I forget and try
To pull a piece off for the taste.

13

Bushfires suggest their bark-dyed hair
In rust-topped scrub, their nails and jewels
In calcined shells, and other signs,
Imagined relics of the race,

In bones baked light and charred stiff fur,
In pitch-black ash that cuts the glare
In fine white sand it mixes with,
Faint cries upon the searing wind.

14

Our darker-than-tar shadows stains
That stick fast on packed melting streets,
I hunger for the sandy wastes
Where people never stay for long

Because they fear the emptiness,
The desiccated skeletons
That in the blinding light rub in
The nothingness their deaths will bring.

15

The bodies of dead birds exposed
To heat, sand, wind and cleansing sea,
It's beautifully unhuman here,

Not rotten with our fear of death.
There's truth in gleaming bone and shell,
In seaweed dried out black and hard.

16

Sky and sea and beach are bare,
As still and silent as a shell.
As ghost-faint as the daytime moon,

A cool breeze thins my heavy flesh
And husk of crab and feather weigh
Upon the lightness of my hand.

17

The sand dunes welcome with their shapes,
The entrances like open arms,
A boneyard glinting where I find

White shells worn thin as wafered bread,
Time stripping me as wind strips rocks,
Salt water leaping clear like flame.

18

The wind has built high walls of sand
And carves out as it blows away
The frescos of an open tomb,
Where men and women come and go

In stories older than the hills,
The same as the Egyptians told:
Our only lasting human theme
The long procession of the dead.